First published 2000 in *The Macmillan Treasury of Nursery Stories*
This collection first published 2010 by Macmillan Children's Books
a division of Macmillan Publishers Limited
20 New Wharf Road, London N1 9RR
Basingstoke and Oxford
Associated companies throughout the world
www.panmacmillan.com

ISBN: 978-0-230-74992-4

MACMILLAN CHILDREN'S BOOKS

Little Red Riding-Hood

and other stories

Retold by
Mary Hoffman

Illustrated by
Anna Currey

Little Red Riding-Hood

There was once a pretty little girl who lived with her mother and father in a country village. Her father was a woodcutter and both her parents and her grandmother loved her better than anything in the world. Her grandmother made her a red cape with a hood such as fine ladies of those days wore when they went riding.

The little girl loved her red cape and wore it so often that everyone called her Little Red Riding-Hood, though her name was Biddy. One day, her mother said to Little Red Riding-Hood, "I want you to visit your grandmother. She hasn't been well so I have made her a dish of custard. Here, it's in this basket with a little butter and some other goodies."

It was a lovely day and Little Red Riding-Hood was happy to go. Her grandmother lived in the next village and she had to walk through a wood but she wasn't afraid. She could hear her father and some other men cutting down trees in the wood. Little Red Riding-Hood sang as she went and would have skipped but she was worried about spilling the custard.

As she walked carefully along the path, all of a sudden a big hairy wolf stepped out in front of her. He would have eaten her up straight away, but he knew the woodcutters were nearby. So he just said, "Where are you going, little girl?"

"To see my grandmother, who isn't well," answered Little Red Riding-Hood. "I am taking her a custard."

"And where does your grandmother live?" asked the wolf, thinking he might get two meals in one.

"It's the first house in the next village," said Little Red Riding-Hood, who was a polite little girl.

So the wolf ran ahead and reached the grandmother's cottage first. He knocked at the door — tock, tock.

"Who's there?" called the grandmother.

The wolf tried to sound like a little girl. "It's me, Granny," he squeaked. "Mummy has sent me with a custard."

The grandmother didn't feel well enough to get up. "Just lift the latch and let yourself in, dear," she said.

So the wolf lifted the latch and bounded into the cottage. He grabbed Little Red Riding-Hood's grandmother and gobbled her up in one big bite.

Meanwhile, Little Red Riding-Hood reached the cottage and knocked at the door — tock, tock.

"Who is it?" came a gruff voice.

"Grandma must have a very bad sore throat," thought the little girl. "It's me, Little Red Riding-Hood," she called out loud.

"Just lift the latch and let yourself in, dear," said the voice.

So Little Red Riding-Hood lifted the latch and let herself in. The curtains were drawn and it was dark inside the cottage but, as the little girl approached the bed, she didn't think her grandmother looked quite right.

"Come closer and give your old Granny a kiss," said the wolf. You see, the wolf had put the grandmother's nightie and bonnet on and had hidden under the bedclothes! Little Red Riding-Hood went closer.

"Oh, Grandma, what big ears you have," she said, looking at the wolf's furry ears.

"All the better to hear you with, my dear," said the wolf.

"Oh, Grandma, what big eyes you have," said Little Red Riding-Hood, seeing the wolf's eyes glittering in the dark.

"All the better to see you with, my dear," said the wolf.

"Oh, Grandma, what big teeth you have," shrieked Little Red Riding-Hood as she looked at the wolf's terrible mouth.

"All the better to EAT you with, my dear!" snarled the wolf and he leapt out of bed and swallowed Little Red Riding-Hood on the spot.

But on the way down his throat she screamed for help so loudly that the woodcutters heard her.

They came rushing to the cottage and the first one, who happened to be Little Red Riding-Hood's father, split the wolf's stomach with his axe. Out came Little Red Riding-Hood. Out came the grandmother. They were not much the worse for wear and they all celebrated their lucky escape.

But the wolf was dead, of course.

Puss in Boots

Once upon a time there was a poor miller who had three sons. When the old man died, he left his sons three things: his mill; his donkey and his cat. Well, the oldest son took the mill, of course, and the second son took the donkey, so the youngest son had to be content with the cat.

The cat was no ordinary one, however, and promised that he would help his new young master to gain a fortune.

"Just get me a pouch to wear round my neck and a

pair of leather boots, and you will see what will happen," said the cat.

So the young miller's son had a pair of leather boots made to fit his cat and a pouch for him to wear round his neck. The cat had a plan, you see, and he put it to work straightaway. He filled the pouch with lettuce and then he went and lay down outside a rabbit-hole and pretended to be dead.

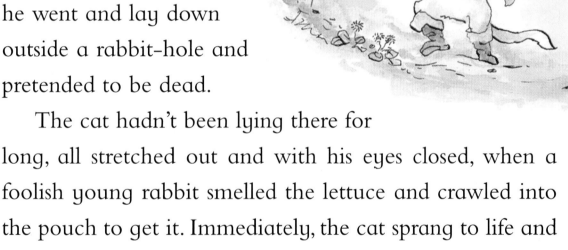

The cat hadn't been lying there for long, all stretched out and with his eyes closed, when a foolish young rabbit smelled the lettuce and crawled into the pouch to get it. Immediately, the cat sprang to life and killed the rabbit. But, instead of bringing it home for his master's supper, he took it to the palace of the king.

"A present from the Marquis of Carabas," he said, standing on his hind legs and laying the rabbit in front of the throne.

"The Marquis of Carabas?" said the king. "I've never heard of him, but I thank him for his kindness."

A week later, the cat put seed in his pouch and caught a pair of plump partridges, using the same trick. He took them to the king, too.

"The Marquis of Carabas presents his compliments," he said to the king, "and offers you this brace of partridges from his estate."

"How kind of the Marquis!" said the king. "Please thank your master for his present."

And so it went on for several months. Every week the clever Puss in Boots would take His Majesty something that he had caught and pretend it was from the Marquis of Carabas.

One day, while he was at the palace, the cat heard that the king was going to take his daughter for a drive by the river. Now this princess was the most beautiful young woman that Puss in Boots had ever seen, and he had been waiting for this moment.

He rushed home and told his master to do as he said and he would win a fortune.

"You must go down to the river tomorrow morning and bathe naked in the water till the king's carriage comes by. Leave all the talking to me."

So, the next day, the miller's son went down to the river and took off his threadbare clothes, which the cat hid under a rock. Then, as soon as he heard the carriage wheels coming, the cat started crying and wringing his paws.

"Help! Help!" he cried. "The Marquis of Carabas is drowning!"

Now, the king recognised the cat who had been bringing him presents for months, saw the young man in the water and ordered his driver to stop.

"Oh, thank you," said Puss in Boots. "Thieves attacked my master and stripped him of his fine clothes. Then they threw him in the river!"

By now, the princess was looking out of the carriage window as well, and saw the miller's son splashing about in the water. She thought he was the best-looking young man she had ever seen.

"Oh, quick, Father, the marquis is drowning! Whatever shall we do?"

The king ordered his footmen to pull the young man out of the water and made one of them give his coat to him. Then he sent another to fetch the finest suit of clothes from the palace—and a towel.

When the young man was dry and dressed, he looked quite handsome enough to be a marquis. The princess smiled at him and the king invited him to join them on their drive.

Puss in Boots ran ahead and

came to a field that was being
harvested. He said to the men
working in the field, "When
the king asks you whose
field this is, you must
say it belongs to the
Marquis of Carabas,
or you will be
chopped into
tiny pieces!"

The cat was so fierce that the workers believed him
and, when the king's carriage came by and the king asked,
"Whose field is this?" they replied, "It belongs to the
Marquis of Carabas, Your Majesty."

"A fine crop you have there," said the king to the
miller's son.

"Yes," said the young man. "That field always does
well."

Puss in Boots ran ahead again and came to an orchard
full of fruit trees. He said to the fruit-pickers, "When the
king asks you whose orchard this is, you must say it
belongs to the Marquis of Carabas, or you will be chopped
into tiny pieces!"

The fruit-pickers were terrified and so, when the king drove by and called out, "Whose orchard is this?" they replied, "It belongs to the Marquis of Carabas, Your Majesty."

The king congratulated the miller's son on his fine harvest of apples and plums, and so it went on. Every field or orchard or fine piece of land they passed seemed to belong to the young marquis and the king was more and more impressed. So was the princess, for she was already in love with the young man's handsome face and she didn't mind at all that he also seemed to be very rich.

Running on ahead, the hard-working cat came to a

castle which belonged to an ogre. He sent in a message that he wished to pay his respects, and the ogre agreed to let him in.

"I have heard," said Puss in Boots, "that you are able to turn yourself into a really large animal, like an elephant. I don't mean to be rude, but I really find it hard to believe."

"Then I'll show you," said the ogre, and he took a deep breath and turned himself into a monstrous lion.

Puss in Boots was terrified and leapt onto the roof,

which was very difficult in boots. He only got down when the ogre returned to his usual shape.

"That was remarkable!" said Puss in Boots. "Now, tell me, can you also make yourself small? For that might be even more difficult."

"Not at all," said the ogre, and straightaway turned himself into a tiny mouse scampering across the floor.

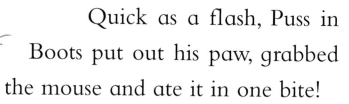

Quick as a flash, Puss in Boots put out his paw, grabbed the mouse and ate it in one bite!

When the king's carriage drew up outside the ogre's castle, there was Puss in Boots at the gate, bowing and greeting the party.

"Welcome to the humble home of my master, the Marquis of Carabas!"

And the miller's son handed the princess down from the carriage and escorted her into the castle, just as if he had lived in it all his life.

There was a fine banquet laid in the dining-hall, because the ogre had been expecting friends to lunch. The miller's son invited the king and princess to join him at the table. And all the ogre's servants were so scared of

Puss in Boots that they didn't say a word. While the king was drinking his wine and eating his cold chicken, he saw how the young people were looking at one another. "How would you like to be my son-in-law, Marquis?" he said.

"Very much indeed," said the young man, smiling, and he was married to the princess the very same day.

Now the clever Puss in Boots lives in luxury and never has to catch mice at all—but he does it sometimes anyway, just for the fun of it.

The Three Wishes

There was once an old woodcutter who was working in the forest. He had his bottle of water and his hunk of bread with him so that he could work all day. Well, as time went by, the woodcutter came to a big old oak tree.

He spat on his hands, picked up his axe and took a swing at the tree trunk. Then he heard a tiny voice saying, "Oh, please don't cut down my home!" and there was a little tree fairy standing at the foot of the great oak.

How she wept and pleaded with him till the old woodcutter, who had never seen a fairy before and was mightily taken with her, thought, "Well, there are plenty of other trees in the forest."

"All right, little one," he said. "I'll not cut your tree."

"Thank you, thank you," said the fairy. "And to show how grateful I am, I shall grant you and your wife your next three wishes." Then she disappeared.

The woodcutter carried on with his work and then went back to his hut, thinking that he must have dreamed what had happened.

"Hullo, wife," he called. "Is my supper ready, for I am mortal hungry."

"No, husband," said his wife. "It won't be ready for another hour."

The woodcutter sat down in his chair and sighed, for he had had nothing but his bread and water since breakfast and it had only been a little bowl of porridge then.

"I wish I had a fine big sausage," he said.

And lo and behold! A savoury, juicy, cooked sausage fell down the chimney!

"What on earth is going on?" asked his wife, very alarmed, for no sausage had ever come tumbling down her chimney before.

Then the woodcutter remembered his "dream". "It must be that fairy's doing," he said, and told his wife the whole story. She was so cross when she realised what had happened.

"What kind of fool are you?" she asked her husband. "You might have wished for gold or a fine house or a carriage, but no—you had to wish for a common or garden sausage such as I might get at the butchers any day. You are such an idiot that I wish that sausage was on your nose!"

And immediately the sausage flew out of the grate and fastened itself to the woodcutter's nose. No matter how he tugged, it would not come off, for it was stuck by magic and that is stronger than any glue.

The woodcutter realised that he was going to have to use his third wish to get the sausage off.

Especially when his wife started to say that it didn't look too bad! Quickly, he made a wish and the sausage came off.

Well, the woodcutter and his wife didn't have any gold or a fine house or carriage. But they did have a big, savoury, juicy sausage and it would have been a shame to waste it. So they sat down and ate it all up. The woodcutter has always kept his eyes open for tree fairies ever since, but he has never been lucky enough to see another one.

The Musicians
of Bremen

There was once a donkey who had worked all his life for a miller but was now getting old. He knew that the miller couldn't afford to keep him as a pet so he decided to set out for the town of Bremen and become a musician there. After all, he could sing a fine "hee-haw!"

On his way he met a dog, lying by the side of the road and panting. "What's the matter?" asked the donkey.

"I've run away from home," said the dog. "I am too old to hunt any more and I think my master was planning to shoot me."

"Then why not come with me?" said the donkey. "I'm going to Bremen to be a musician. You could do that, too. You know how to howl, I suppose?"

When the dog had recovered, the two new friends walked on towards Bremen. After a short while they came across a cat sitting on the path looking very sorry for itself.

"What's the matter?" they asked.

"My teeth are not as sharp as they were and I've lost the taste for catching mice, so my mistress has thrown me out."

"Then come with us to Bremen," said the donkey and the dog. "We are going to be musicians and you could join us. We know how tunefully cats sing at night."

Not long after this the three companions passed a farm and there sat a cock on the gatepost, crowing with all his might.

"It's not morning," said the other animals. "Why are you crowing now?"

"I heard my mistress say I was getting too old. I am supposed to be turned into stew tomorrow, so I'm singing as much as I can today."

"Well, bring your fine singing voice to Bremen with us," said the others. "Wouldn't you rather be a musician than end up in the pot?"

The cock agreed and the four friends went on their way. When night fell, they settled in a wood. The donkey and the dog lay at the foot of a tree, while the cat climbed up into its branches and the cock flew right to the top.

While he was up there, the cock saw a distant light. He flew down to tell his friends.

"I think there's a house over there. Perhaps we could find better lodging and maybe some food?"

So they set off towards the light. It came from a very cosy house on the edge of the wood. The donkey, being the tallest, looked in at the window and came back to tell them what he had seen.

"It's a robbers' house," he said. "They are all sitting round a table and it is absolutely loaded with good things to eat and drink."

So the four friends made a plan. The donkey went back to the window and the dog climbed up on his back and the cat sat on the dog's shoulders, while the cock perched on the cat's head. Then they gave their first concert.

The donkey hee-hawed, the dog howled, the cat

caterwauled and the cock crowed "cock-a-doodle-doo!"
They all burst through the window at the same time and
the robbers were so terrified of the noise, thinking it must
be a ghost, that they ran away
into the woods.

The four friends had a very good
meal of the robbers' food and then
settled down to sleep in the places
that suited them best. The
donkey lay on some straw in
the yard. The dog slept behind
the door, the cat curled up
near the remains of the
fire and the cock flew
up into the rafters.

The robbers began
to get over their fright
and sent one member
of the gang back to
the house to see
what was going on.
In he crept, but the
house was in

darkness now, so he thought he would light a taper at the fire. He mistook the cat's eyes for two burning coals and poked the taper at them.

The cat shrieked and flew at the man's face, scratching him with her claws. He stumbled over the dog by the door, who bit him in the leg. He ran out into the yard, where the donkey kicked him hard and the cock flew down from the rafters crowing "cock-a-doodle-doo!"

The robber got back to his friends in a terrible state.

"There's a dreadful witch in the house," he cried. "She scratched me and cursed me. And then a man with a knife stabbed me in the leg as I was coming out of the door and a monster was waiting in the yard, who beat me with a wooden club! And then a judge called from up on the roof—'There's nothing you can do!'—so I ran away as fast as I could."

When his companions saw the robber's scratches and bruises, no one dared go back to the house. So the four friends lived there in happiness to the end of their days and never reached Bremen at all.